THE GOLDEN BOOK OF DEATH

BY MICHAEL DAHL

ILLUSTRATED BY SERG SOULEIMAN

Librarian Reviewer
Laurie K. Holland
Media Specialist

Reading Consultant
Elizabeth Stedem
Educator/Consultant

Raintree

Raintree is an imprint of Capstone Global Library Limited, a
company incorporated in England and Wales having its registered
office at 7 Pilgrim Street, London, EC4V 6LB – Registered
company number: 6695582

"Raintree" is a registered trademark of Pearson Education
Limited, under licence to Capstone Global Library Limited

Text © Stone Arch Books, 2009
First published by Stone Arch Books in 2008
First published in hardback in the United Kingdom in 2009
The moral rights of the proprietor have been asserted.

Senior Designer for Cover and Interior: Kay Fraser
Graphic Designer: Brann Garvey
Edited in the UK by Laura Knowles
Printed and bound in China by Leo Paper Products Ltd

ISBN 978-1406212761 (hardback)

13 12 11 10 09
10 9 8 7 6 5 4 3 2 1

British Library Cataloguing in Publication Data
Dahl, Michael.
The golden book of death. -- (Library of doom)
813.5'4-dc22
A full catalogue record for this book is available
from the British Library.

TABLE OF CONTENTS

The Library of Doom is the world's largest collection of strange and dangerous books. The Librarian's duty is to keep the books from falling into the hands of those who would use them for evil purposes.

CHAPTER 1

THE BREAK-IN!

An alarm bell is <u>ringing</u> in the Library of Doom.

Someone has **broken in!**

The Librarian stands at the
window of his room.

He listens to the `bell`.

He knows where the <u>sound</u> is coming from.

The alarm is ringing in one of the **deepest corners** of the Library.

The Librarian opens the window
and <u>steps</u> out.

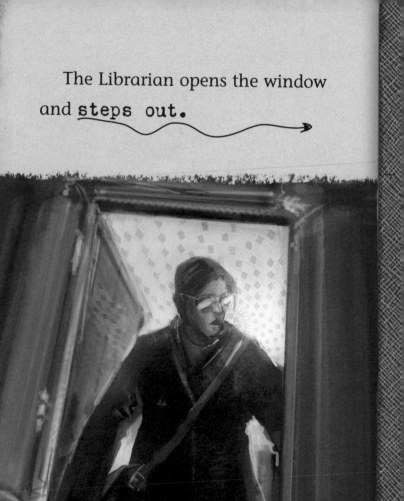

He rushes towards the ringing
alarm bell.

He must find and stop the
intruder.

CHAPTER 2

THE CELL

The Librarian is the guardian of the Library of Doom.

His duty is to keep the Library's books out of evil hands.

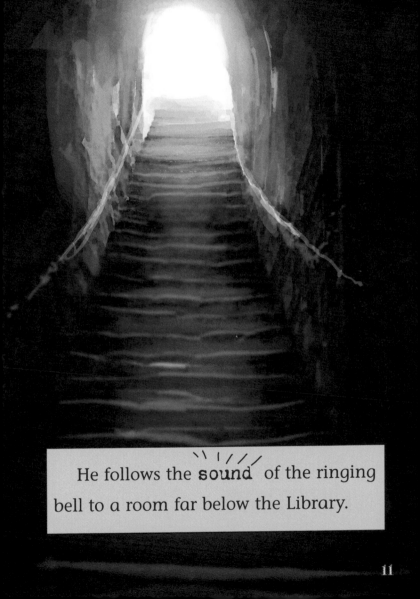

He follows the **sound** of the ringing
bell to a room far below the Library.

The room is an **ancient**
`prison cell.`

Long ago, the room was used for locking up book thieves.

As soon as the Librarian steps into the cell, the bell stops ringing.

He hears another sound.

A metal book **flies out** of a **dark** corner.

The book **hits** the Librarian.

He falls.

{ CHAPTER 3 }

THE GOLDEN BOOK

When the Librarian wakes up,
he is staring at <u>the ceiling</u>.

The Librarian is <u>chained</u> to a **huge** golden book.

His wrists and ankles are held in place by **golden letters.**

A **shadowy figure** moves out of the corner. It is the Librarian's <u>enemy</u>, the Eraser.

"This cell will be your prison," says the Eraser.

"You will never again stop me from destroying or erasing books."

"You won't get away with this," the Librarian tells the Eraser.

"Someone will find me."

"It will be **too late**," says the
Eraser.

"Too late?" asks the Librarian.

"Too late for what?"

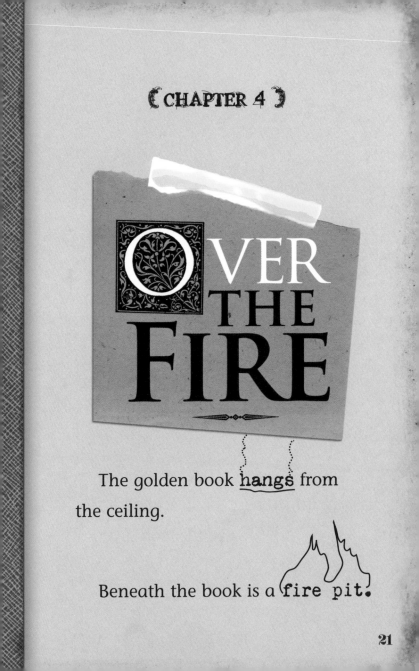

(CHAPTER 4)

OVER THE FIRE

The golden book <u>hangs</u> from the ceiling.

Beneath the book is a fire pit.

The Eraser has filled the pit with

old books.

"Old books are good for <u>burning</u>," says the Eraser.

Then he laughs and lights the
fire pit.

The Librarian smells the
burning paper.

"Nothing can help you now," says the Eraser.

ha ha ha ha ha ha ha

Then he {laughs} and walks out of the room.

CHAPTER 5

THE BLANK PAGE

The Librarian cannot reach any of his pockets.

They hold **special books** and tools that could help him escape.

The Librarian **struggles** against the golden letters.

It is no use. They are too **strong**.

The golden book grows **warm**.

The Librarian can feel the **heat** against his back and legs.

Suddenly, he begins to **shake.**

A small piece of paper falls out of his sleeve.

The **paper** **rolls** into his **hand**.

Quickly, his fingers open the paper.

Nothing is written on it. The paper is **blank**.

"The Eraser is right," says the Librarian to himself. "Nothing will help me now."

The blank page glows softly.

It pulls the golden letters from the (chains) onto its blank surface.

The letters form a word. FREE.

The Librarian's hands and feet
are free.

He leaps off the golden book and
puts out the fire.

"All blank pages wish to be
filled with letters," says the
Librarian.

Then he rushes out of the room,
in search of the **Eraser**.

✺ THE END ✺

A PAGE FROM THE LIBRARY OF DOOM

GOLD

Gold has been admired for its colour and its beauty ever since humans began to dig for metals in the earth. Gold was also prized for its ability to last. The shiny metal is not affected by rain, heat, or cold. Gold will not rust or tarnish either.

Gold is one of the softest metals on Earth. It can easily be pounded or stretched into different sizes and shapes. One ounce of gold can be hammered into a thread that will stretch for 50 miles (80 kilometers)!

One ounce of gold can also be pounded into a thin sheet large enough to cover the floor of the average school classroom.

The deepest gold mine in the world is the **Savuka** (sah-VOO-kuh) mine in South Africa. Miners can travel more than 3 kilometres (2 miles) underground!

Gold artwork has been found in ancient Egyptian tombs over 5,000 years old.

Thin pieces of gold, known as gold leaf, are used to decorate special religious paintings known as **icons** (EYE-konz). Icons are found in Russian and Greek Orthodox churches.

Some people believe gold has magical healing powers. People drink a mixture of water and gold dust as a remedy for sickness and disease. Luckily, gold has no taste, and it will pass through the body without harming it!

ABOUT THE AUTHOR

Michael Dahl is the author of more than
100 books for children and young adults.
He has twice won the AEP Distinguished
Achievement Award for his non-fiction. His
Finnegan Zwake mystery series was chosen
by the Agatha Awards to be among the
five best mystery books for children in 2002
and 2003. He collects books on poison and
graveyards, and lives in a haunted house in
Minneapolis, USA.

ABOUT THE ILLUSTRATOR

Serg Souleiman lives and works in Carlsbad,
California, USA, as a designer and
illustrator.

GLOSSARY

ancient (AYN-shuhnt) – something that is very, very old

cell (SEL) – a small room, often used for holding criminals

guardian (GAR-dee-uhn) – a person who is in charge of protecting something

intruder (in-TROOD-uhr) – someone who has broken into a place where they are not wanted

shadowy (SHAD-oh-ee) – being dark and often mysterious

thieves (THEEVZ) – people who steal things

DISCUSSION QUESTIONS

1. The Librarian is responsible for keeping the Library's books out of evil hands. What types of things are you responsible for? How do you make sure the job gets done?

2. The Librarian risks his life to protect the books inside the Library of Doom. Do you own anything that you would try to save, even if it was risky? What would you save and why?

3. This story leaves you wondering what will happen next. Do you like stories that have this type of open ending, or would you rather have the author wrap everything up? Explain your answer.

WRITING PROMPTS

1. At the end of the story, the Librarian chases after the Eraser. Pretend you are the author and write another chapter about what happens next.

2. The books inside the Library of Doom are important to the Librarian. What is the most important book to you? Describe why you like the book and why it's your favourite.

3. The Librarian says, "All blank pages wish to be filled with letters." Grab a blank sheet of paper, and write a scary story that fills the entire page with words.

MORE BOOKS TO READ

This story may be over, but there are many more dangerous adventures in store for the Librarian. Will the Librarian be able to escape the cave of the deadly giant bookworms? Will he defeat the rampaging Word Eater in time to save the world? You can only find out by reading the other books from the Library of Doom...